AF437677

# Ai Jiang's
# Smol Tales From Between Worlds

Tales From Between Presents

# SMOL TALES FROM BETWEEN WORLDS

TALES FROM BETWEEN

London

www.talesfrombetween.wordpress.com

Copyright © 2023 by Tales From Between

All rights reserved.

Cover Image by Terablete. Cover Design by Matthew Stott.

# Contents

# About

**Tales From Between Presents** is a journal dedicated to the work of a single author each edition. Each mini-collection will feature a handful of short stories, author notes, and an interview. This publication is edited by author and publisher, Matthew Stott.

**CONTACT:** frombetween@gmail.com

**TWITTER:** @from_between

**PATREON:** Join our Patreon and support this publication. It also acts as an eBook subscription to everything we publish. Support new writing: patreon.com/TalesFromBetween

# Meet The Author

Ai Jiang is a Chinese-Canadian writer and an immigrant from Fujian. She is a member of HWA, SFWA, and Codex. Her work can be found in F&SF, The Dark, Uncanny, among others. She is the recipient of Odyssey Workshop's 2022 Fresh Voices Scholarship and the author of *Linghun*. Find her on Twitter (@AiJiang_) and online (http://aijiang.ca).

You can usually find her hunched over her desk, munching on snacks that she shouldn't be eating or drinking far too many bubble teas while insisting that watching movies and shows on Netflix is a part of her "research"—active procrastination—for her writing.

# The Rabbits

R abbits ran across the front of our lawn daily. But one day, they lay unmoving amid the tall grass.

Every morning, my son and I would walk to the train station together. Usually, there was small talk between us. Sometimes it was about the weather; sometimes it was about the news; often, it was about the dead rabbits we found on our lawn. And sometimes, we refrained from mentioning the rabbits but acknowledged their presence in silence instead.

When we reached the train station, we would stop in front of the entrance. I'd wait quietly as my son adjusted his hat. Then, he would adjust his tie so that it was tighter, even though it was already tight enough. When he finished with this daily ritual, we would walk into the station without looking at one another. We would stop in the middle of the station and face each other.

"Here," I would say as I handed him a banknote.

There would be a pause before he took the note from my hand.

"Do you need another?" I would ask.

He stared down, not at me, but at the opened purse I clutched in my hands. My son would stare hard at the purse without meeting my eyes. He also did this with the rabbits before we started our walk. His hands would ball up in the pocket where he placed the note I had given him. I would not hesitate as my weathered hands plunged back into my purse. This was the least I could do. I knew that he would not ask for a second, but I also knew that he needed it.

It was like this every day: the walk, the ritual, the handing of the note at the station, and sometimes, a second handing of a second note. Then, I would leave as he headed to the platform to wait for his train to work. I would stand at the entrance of the station for a while before I headed home.

Today, there are no longer dead rabbits on my lawn. I walk alone to the train station. I pause in front of the station entrance and look beside me where my son should have been standing and wait the amount of time he usually took to complete his ritual. I look past the shadow of my son and see my husband's shadow beside him, adjusting the watch on his wrist although it is already tight enough before he checks for the time. When they are done, the three of us walk to the middle of the station together.

Today, a man is waiting for me. My husband and son's shadows disappear as I approach him. He hands me a document and leaves to catch the incoming train. I fold it and place it into my opened purse, devoid of bank notes, before leaving the station. I do not pause before I head home where I lay on my empty lawn, unblinking.

*Previously published in MYRIAD.*

### *AUTHOR NOTE*

I had written this story for a contest, but it hadn't placed. We were given a photo prompt of an old woman, perhaps upper middle class, who was handing an envelope of sorts to a man right before the platforms of a train station. The image was in sepia. I had written the piece while thinking about a struggling man who needed to pay off his debt, and his mother trying to help him as much as she could, given that the man's father, her husband, had passed trying to repay a debt of his own. With the imagery of rabbits, I find they always appear when it comes to hinting at symbolic innocence. And that's what I wanted the readers to understand. They are in debt, they are struggling, they are trying their best, and they are innocent but hunted by the economy's relentless predations.

# The Catcher
# in the Eye

CW: Sexual harassment, graphic imagery

I kept my right eye closed because I saw ghosts through it. My parents thought they were imaginary friends I would soon outgrow—they weren't. But what did they know?

"One—or two?" my optometrist asked, switching lenses.

"Two," I said. He repeated the process until I could recite the letters on the eye exam chart a few feet in front of me. To him, there were only letters, but through my right eye, there was a woman—translucent—in clothing stained by dried blood below the hips, smiling. In her hands sat a child's head. I closed my eye.

"Please keep both eyes open for the exam," said the optometrist.

My breaths stopped, and I opened my right eye. I screamed as the woman's face, merged with the child's in a strange blurring of features, appeared before the lenses, shuddering momentarily before fuzzing like a static channel.

I squeezed my eyes shut, throat burning, tears drenching the neck of my shirt. This wasn't the first time this had happened, but the other times were bearable—the visions weren't as clear. It had only been a month since the ghosts appeared, but it felt like it had been years.

Before leaving, I paused by the entrance, listening to my parents' whispers. Mother clutched Father's arm.

"Well, what are we supposed to *do* about it?" Mother said.

"I'm not sure I'm qualified to offer advice on this... perhaps a specialist," said my optometrist.

Behind my parents stood the woman with the child's head in her hands—the faces no longer merged. She squeezed then stretched the child's face, the skin looking far too elastic.

In a photo pinned up in my mother's room, she cradled my newborn self on the hospital bed, smiling though her gown was soiled. She was smiling, but there was so much blood.

The woman stepped into my mother's body, disappearing. And the child's head floated towards me, its mishappen mouth ajar, mouthing, "Remember me?"

My parents never brought me to the optometrist again.

I didn't want to see the ghosts, but *they* wanted to see *me*.

Later that night, my mother tossed me an eyepatch made of beige silk. "Here, just wear this for now. It should help with your... issues." She swirled the glass of wine in her hand, a drop spilt over the side, dropping onto the red loveseat. A tight smile flashed across both our faces, teeth clenched so tight I was surprised they didn't all fall out. So similar. I stopped smiling. The fabric of the eyepatch felt rough in my hand, like it had been used for a long while before.

In the bathroom mirror, the edges of the fabric seemed to dissolve into my skin, making it appear as though I only had one eye. Blending in wasn't a possibility now.

"Why don't you just put her in therapy?" Father asked.

"I never went to therapy, and I turned out fine," Mother said, glaring from the corner of her eye.

"Well, did you see things, too?" Though he answered, his eyes stayed glued to his work computer, finding far more interest in his never-ending emails rather than his family. It was how he was raised. I hoped he didn't expect the same from me.

Mother hesitated for a moment before the smile re-emerged on her face. "N-no, of course not." Then her face hardened once more as she tsked. "Besides, what do you think the ladies at my book club would say if they found out our daughter went to therapy."

Mother rose from her spot, walked over to where I hovered by the living room entrance with a lipstick in her hand. "Here, this might help." She waved her arms as if conducting an orchestra. "Cover up, if you will."

She wasn't trying to be funny, but I couldn't see how lipstick would help me be more 'normal'.

"When I was your age, all the girls wore it," Mother said. Her hands shook as she painted the red over my lips, her eyes blank, as though recalling something she didn't want to remember.

I noticed a lipstick stain on her front teeth, but I didn't dare mention it: she hated when she didn't look perfect. I let my gaze drop, focusing on her black leather heels instead. It was the fifth pair she'd purchased this month. "Margret has them. The cheaper version, of course," she had said.

Picture day would be a few days before junior year started.

"It's fine. Just take it off for pictures," Father said, gesturing absently to the eyepatch.

He made it sound so easy, though his own pictures took hours because he couldn't stand his tie sitting even slightly askew in the photos. He took a deep breath, adjusted his tie, his eyes still glued to the screen. Even asleep, my father never took off his tie. I wondered if he might choke one day. I wondered if he already had.

In the bathroom, I ran my fingers ran along the edges of the eyepatch, lifting the corner briefly. A small child, perhaps five, sat next to my leg. It clung onto my calf. Its arms were two times too long for its body, ending in sharpened black nails attached to unjointed fingers. The child sank its claws into my flesh. There was no head on its body.

I left the sink running to help drown out laughter bubbling up my throat.

There were razor nicks and the swollen pores of ingrown hairs scattered across my skin. The magazines my mom read said *women* needed to shave their legs for greater 'sex appeal'—I guess sex appeal could be a necessary thing at sixteen, but who really cares? What did the magazine say about the men? My father didn't care for magazines; it was always about the papers. But even then, he sometimes stared at the businessmen and politicians, then cleared his throat, tightened his tie.

I ran my razor under the water, the scent of shaving cream—fruity and synthetic—attacked my nose as I ran the blade over areas already shaved, over and over and over—

I didn't feel pain from the nails, or the rawness of my skin, screaming from the razor. Yet a whimper made its way out before I yanked the eyepatch back down, pressing it into my eye until I saw white specks floating across my vision. Poor child, poor me.

I moved the blade up over my armpits. Tanks tops were trending now. Not that I cared, really.

"Are you ready?" Mother called from downstairs.

No. "Yeah."

At the bottom of the stairs, Mother puts on an automatic smile, raising an arm mechanically with lipstick gripped in her hand like a knife. She sliced my lips rouge.


I waited until the last minute to take off the eyepatch when I sat down on the seat in front of the photographer and his oversized camera. He walked over to adjust my position. I felt suddenly conscious of how red and unnatural my lips must have looked. The lipstick from Mother felt weighted in my pocket.

"Tilt your head up, good... good," he said, too close to my ear. His breath reeked of alcohol—the same scent that wafted from my father's breath after dinner, where he chugged, and chugged, and chugged, and—

Behind the photographer, a twig-bodied girl danced in a white tutu—a tragic white dove. Her body resembled the small wooden figurines in the art class I took—and failed—her features scraped and carved. She twirled and twirled and twirled—

Her steps light compared to my heavy footfalls since puberty.

"Maybe dancing isn't quite... *fitting*," Mother had said. I had loved it. But she made me hate it. "Looks like we both aren't cut out to be swans, huh?"

"Now turn your body this way..." The photographer's hand lingered at the crook of my waist. My muscles tensed, and I held my breath.

"Relax..."

"Excuse me, sir. Could you hurry it up?" came the voice of a snooty girl with a flat nose, who poked her head behind the curtain obscuring the waiting area. She gave me a once over and scoffed, adjusting her tube top only to have it dip down again.

The photographer sighed and moved away. I exhaled slowly, my lips quivering.

Was it the lipstick? I would never wear it again.

He showed me the pictures when he was finished, and he could tell I wasn't pleased. The excessive rouge lips stuck out from my pale face, and my smile was more of a grimace. The ballerina cackled behind me, leaning in to take a look.

"Perfect," she whispered, sarcastic. I wondered if the photographer could hear her. "Mother would love it, wouldn't she?"

I frowned, not at the photo, but at the ballerina. The photographer must have thought it was the former because he said, "Don't worry, we'll edit the photo so everything looks... better. And if you want, you can always filter it if you plan on posting it on social media."

It was fine. Student IDs are meant to be ugly. Social media is a lie. My parents never bought these photos—not that I wanted them.

"Thanks, I will." I smiled, showing all my teeth. I wished they looked as pointed as the child's nails. That would be much better than lipstick any day.

I put my eyepatch back on.

On my way out, I looked back at the photographer. His mask was almost as thick as my mother's cake—a murky, shadowed mass encapsulating his head. I swiped a hand across my lips. A smear of rouge marked my skin.

During March break, Mother shoved a flyer she found stuffed in our mailbox by someone from our neighbourhood in front of me. It was posted by a lady living down the street. "I know you weren't great at dancing, but what about piano? It's *nearly* as elegant. Plus, you won't need your legs."

We both stared down at my large calves and wide thighs. Mother nodded. "Yes, piano will do. But maybe also veganism? You could try it. Better for your health."

Someone should stop her from reading all these false articles and pop culture magazines with the models on the covers. I pinched my skin. My diet wasn't particularly unhealthy—not that Mother allowed for anything unhealthy anyhow—and I still exercised. Did I really need to lose weight? Maybe. I hunched forward, hoping it would make me seem smaller.

"Stand up straight," my mother barked.

She plucked my eyepatch from my eye. Behind her, a large shadow hovered. "You haven't washed this in weeks. Let me run it through with the laundry. You can keep your eye closed until then."

I did what I was told and watched with one eye as Mother trudged down the hall, but the shadow stayed, merging with my limbs, adding to my flesh, making me notice the protrusions and stretch marks I ignored previously, under my baggy clothing. But in an instant, it dripped away, melting onto the ground like a puddle and following my mother before becoming one with her body, revealing in shadow protrusions what her Botox and tummy tuck treatments desperately tried to hide.

I opened my eye again, wondering if I'd closed the wrong one. I hadn't.


Father dropped me off at the steps of the piano lady's house when spring came around. There were too many flowers in her front yard, each grouped by type: roses, lilies, sunflowers. I picked a rose and snapped off the stem, its thorns nicking my finger before I tossed it aside. I made my way up the cobbled pathway, placing the flower into my pocket for safekeeping, careful not the crinkle its petals, then wiped the blood on my new jeans. I hated them, but Mother insisted sweatpants would "simply not do."

"Hello, you must be Ino," said a stout woman with large, round glasses, magnifying her pupils so they looked like the eyes of a fly. The glasses left barely any of her bronzed face uncovered around it. Or maybe she didn't need glasses that big at all and just wanted her eyes to look bigger, like my mother who always wore bulky contacts without a prescription. I had glasses, too, but they made the ghosts more pronounced. Squinting was bearable, most of the time—until someone laughed about it in school.

"Yes," was the only thing I could think to say since my father hadn't told me the woman's name.

"Wedda. You can call me Wedda," she said, as if reading my mind. "Come along."

Wedda didn't spare a second and grabbed me by the shoulders, pushing me inside. Before she seated me in front of the piano, she gazed at my hands.

"They look just like mine when I was younger," she said, then rested herself on a rocking chair next to the aged wooden instrument. Her perfume smelt of dead flowers and disinfectant. Around her neck hung far too many pearls. From this angle, it was clear her bronzed face was unnatural—too much foundation of the wrong colour or maybe a spray tan: A cake face like mother.

My mind swam as my fingers ran over the black and white keys, playing various scales in a disjointed manner, awkward, unfamiliar—my fingers tripping and stumbling over, and over, and over, and—

Wedda repeated words I didn't understand every time I played the wrong note. I was only a beginner—why did she insist on making me play what she knew I couldn't?

"I won several awards when I was younger. Never made these mistakes even though I started playing when I was two." She shot me a scrutinizing stare. "Why don't you take that eyepatch off? Maybe you'll make fewer errors," Wedda said.

I shook my head. I played the wrong note—again—and my fingers withdrew from the piano with a sudden jerk.

"*I* was such a quick learner. Soared through the levels. A piano prima donna if you will!" Wedda shook her head. "This simply *won't* do."

She reached over and took my eyepatch off.

"Now look at that. Isn't that much better? Maybe you need *rouge* on those lips... When I was performing, I wore the most striking dresses. The lips were never bare!" Wedda winked. "Appearance was also part of the performance, you know?"

It took a few seconds before my vision adjusted. Small white specks littered the front of my eyes. The piano sat rotting in front of me with its only redeeming feature the horrendous satin covering—only because it was not as decayed. Wedda must have used it to hide its age and mold. Spider webs sat at the edges of its frame. Wormwood beetles scuttled in and out of gaping holes.

"Well, don't stop. Continue!" Wedda said.

I slammed my hands against the keys, making Wedda flinch in her seat, mouth dropping open. A smile stretched across my face, as polite as can be. "Thank you, but I best get going now."

When I left, I didn't bother putting my eyepatch back on. Without it, the flowers outside became carnivorous traps, snapping at my heels, begging me to notice them. Ignoring the ghosts didn't help them go away. They would always be there. Better to get used to them than pretend. Why pretend, anyway?

I kept my eyepatch off. I saw clearer this way.

Weeds peeked out from under the flowers, their spiked edges jutted. The tiny ghosts of all of Wedda's students, who left despising her, huddled around the roots of the weeds for comfort, mewing their sorrows my way.

Poor them.

The terrible woman only seemed to project her past onto her students, and I didn't want any of that. I thought of my mother's scrutinizing gaze and how she wrinkled her nose every time she saw me. Like her, I was a twig-like child. But I wasn't anymore, and she hated that because she was the same.

There were always cliques at school. I wasn't a fan, but maybe I should have tried harder to join one. Maybe it would've made life easier. *Connections*, my father said, *are the key to life*. But what I heard was *fake friends—get yourself some fake friends who can help you and then become a fake friend, too.*

Each of the girls and boys sitting together in groups at lunch had a strange ghost tethered to their heads like a balloon with the string pulled taut upwards. A replica of their faces only without all the makeup, without all the smiles, and without all the feigned confidence. I looked above me. My own balloon had a smile stretched wide like the Cheshire Cat's. Why did my balloon look so much more sinister?

The group noticed me looking and sneered, turning up their noses. I continued staring anyway.

These ghosts weren't really ghosts, but sometimes, I wished they were.

One girl sitting at the edge of the crowd ducked her head, embarrassed. We shared a brief look, but for once, I felt understanding. The balloon above her head sat deflated, trailing near the ground. I wondered if my mother's balloon would have looked the same when she was younger.

The same photographer returned to take pictures at the end of year dance, but the ballerina was no longer behind him. Instead, there was my balloon, chomping at the air above his head, running its tongue over the sharpened teeth that had grown in over the year. Wouldn't it be lovely to snap off his head? Wouldn't it be lovely if I—

He approached me with the same slow, upright crawl as before. "Tilt your—"

"Sorry, you're a little too close," I said, leaning back, offering him the most reproachful and disgusted look I could muster. My conversed feet shuffled backwards. Mother failed to get me in heels for the first time. The shoes cost me a chunk of my savings, but it was worth it.

The photographer frowned and straightened, clearing his throat. My balloon closed its lips over his face, teeth thrashing at his features.

"Say cheese," he murmured, eyeing the next girl peeking through the curtains the whole time like she was lunch.


I quit piano after a handful of lessons, and I never did start that diet Mother pushed so hard onto me. Mother didn't stop trying, even though her shadow continued to grow every time she came back from the surgeon's.

I always wondered why my father never had ghosts lingering around him, but I wouldn't be surprised if he was already one himself. Nothing was more grotesque than he.

At dinner, I held back a gag when my father's udon splashed against his pressed white shirt and continued to accumulate as he shovelled into his mouth the fish hovering in the soup, speaking, boasting without noticing. His tie stayed clean, pressed.

Mother was too invested in cutting pieces of thick noodles into small pieces. She didn't want to have to move her face since the bandages bounded much of it far too tight. Why didn't she just cook congee instead? I cringed at the high-pitched squeal escaping her lips when she stretched her mouth too wide. Her fork and knife clattered onto the china. I flinched. Father ate and spoke without a pause.

The child still clung to my leg. The head from the optometrist had left the woman's hands and attached itself to its original body, but I hadn't noticed until now. I'd almost become used to its presence until it squawked. The child mimicked my mother, mocking and laughing in response. Then its eyes met mine. Bandages appeared across its face before disappearing, revealing features far too symmetrical and perfect to be mine. I looked away. If I stared too long, maybe I'd want perfection, too.

My father spent the entire dinner building up to the announcement of what was no doubt his promotion while my mother talked over him, bragging about her new hair and shopping hauls. This was his third promotion this year. I suspect he was only trying to get attention, acknowledgement, not that our attention would've been enough for him; not that any of us would have noticed or cared.

I stood up in the middle of my father's overused speech without finishing my food, letting my chair topple onto the floor behind me with a crunch—wood against wood. My udon sat bloated within the bowl clutched between my hands. The flesh of the fish collected at the bottom with the bones floating on top. I poured it down the sink and heard my mother mutter a comment about wasting food, then rescinded it when she realized that it would help lose inches off my waistline.

Before I left the kitchen, I looked back for a brief moment and saw panic in my father's eyes as he, in haste, launched into speaking about another recent achievement of his.

Without sparing another glance, I headed outside to the end of the driveway where our trash cans sat. I pulled the crumpled eyepatch from my pocket and threw it into the green bin, then took out the crumbled rose from my other pocket—most of the pieces moldy and stuck to the inner pocket of the jeans I'd only worn twice and never washed since Mother purchased them. I pried it from my fingertips, flicking it onto the grounds. Its beauty suffocated, gone.

Hidden in the hollowed sole of each of my shoes were a few cigarettes and a small lighter. I pulled them out. Mother often searched my room for 'inappropriate' items thinking I wouldn't notice, but she always left a mess of things. It was hard not to notice.

They were really all phonies, weren't they?

*And what about you?* My balloon laughed.

I lit my cigarette, took a drag, blew smoke in the balloon's direction, then chucked it at its head.

I wrapped my arms around myself. The small child who held on to my leg no longer looked sinister but resembled an unedited childhood picture of myself I'd lost when we moved. All our family pictures were edited now, printed out and decorated by Mother.

My balloon floated down towards the child, cooing before spreading its lips and swallowing her whole. But the child didn't disappear. She took on the smile of the balloon, its broad grin stretching across more than half her face.

The child's screechy laugh mixed with the balloon's lower cackle. "You're just *perfect*, aren't you?" Again, its mouth widened, stretched until it looked as though it would rip apart. Its eyes stared at me, taunting, beckoning me to step into its cavern.

"What are you doing?" Mother's voice drifted from behind.

Without turning, I tried to hide the cigarettes and lighter, but my mother caught my hand. She swiped a cigarette and lit it without looking at me. To my surprise, Mother unravelled the bandages from her face and threw it into the trash can, over my eyepatch, then blew smoke towards the streetlight. The dull yellow glow emphasized the oil accumulating from her pores and the unhealed, swollen surgery lines carved into her face as she drew in her brows, wincing, but deep in thought.

I didn't answer her, but I didn't need to. We stood in silence, watching the faint white tendrils disappear above us. But it was only for a moment because Father came crashing outside, thudding footsteps stumbling in our direction, shattering the silence. Below me, the child had disappeared, but her laughter remained.

Above my mother's head hovered a balloon not dissimilar to mine. Perhaps we weren't so different after all, and perhaps that was okay.

*Previously published in The Dark.*

### *AUTHOR NOTE*

Many if not most teens are no strangers to body dysmorphia, and with this piece, I wanted to highlight that fact but add in a supernatural bent. Our inner critics are harsh, if not harsher than the external critics within our lives—family, friends, coworkers, employees. To make peace with either is a difficult feat. But to understand that we are not alone in these worries is important, and to understand it enough that we don't push our insecurities onto others is a goal we need to strive for.

# Questions From Between

# BACKSTORY

**Where did you grow up? Do you think it influenced your writing in any identifiable way?**

From birth to around the age of four, I grew up in China in a province called Fujian. I mainly stayed with my mother's family in the city of Changle, but often visited my father's family in a rural village called Shanghu. From age four onwards, I lived in downtown Toronto before moving to Scarborough, Ontario, and now I'm in Markham. I often find myself drawing on my childhood home's landscape in my writing, particularly when it comes to writing about migration or identity.

**Did you have a favourite book as a child?**

I suppose it wasn't one book but The Owls of Ga'Hoole series.

**Do you recall when you first decided you wanted to write stories?**

Looking back, I think I've always wanted to write stories and be a writer. I loved reading growing up, even though it started with my sneaky attempts to buy books through school Scholastic book orders so I can get the toys that accompanied the books. But the more I read, the more I wanted to create and live in my own worlds. As a child, I wanted to write fantastical escapist stories. Now, I want to write stories that are both entertaining but also make a difference. So in my long ramble, I guess I decided I wanted to write stories from the moment I picked up a book, but I wanted to study craft and the art of stories and make it a career in the recent two years.

**You've mentioned before that it was difficult to persuade people close to you that writing was the correct path for you, was it hard to move forward with that lack of firm support?**

It was, but I've always been a persistent and stubborn person growing up, and one thing I've realized I've always done—as do many children I suppose—is to do the exact opposite of what my parents want. They wanted me to make writing a hobby, but I wanted to make writing a career. At first, it was difficult because I knew my income would plummet if I chose to take this path, but as many of those who have followed along my journey so far know, I'm a firm believer that hard work does pay off, and the harder I work, hopefully, the more "successful" I'll become.

**What do those close to you think about your writing now that you are becoming more successful?**

There are definitely more people I know in real life who read my writing now. But I think there's still the belief that one might become some kind of multi-millionaire as soon as you publish a book, which most of us writers understand isn't true. I think there's become an even greater need to push harder, though not so much to show others I can succeed (that's part of it I suppose), but to show how much I'm willing to fight for what I love. I do think it shows, and I've received much more support since.

**You've sold an incredible number of stories in a relatively short amount of time, was there a particular story sale, or venue acceptance, that gave you confidence that yes, you had a real future as a writer?**

There are markets that some might deem more "prestigious" than others, whether it's because of the exposure they offer or the amount they pay. I think there are three venue acceptances that gave me more confidence as a writer: The Magazine of Fantasy and Science Fiction, The Dark, and The Masters Review. Because I like to write across genres, I never know when I might be succeeding in those genres, but since publishing a piece of science fiction, dark fantasy/horror, and non-spec literary fiction in each of those venues, it somehow validated that perhaps I can write after all and that I can appeal to a broad range of audiences, even if I still have a long way to go and much to improve.

**Looking back, is there anything you'd do differently if you were starting again as a writer?**

I don't think there is anything I'd do differently, but not just because of my motto of never having regrets. I think everything happens for a reason, and in every journey, there will be more struggle than smooth paths—if any—and more often than not, opportunities will come at the right moments.

# The Year of
the Niú

On the eve of the Year of the Niú, the animals who won The Great Race, organized thousands of years ago, and their descendants, gathered for a night of festivities. But this day always brought on an unspoken foreignness for the two-headed ox.

The animals had spread out around the world but always returned to the starting line of The Great Race before the New Year.

With Grandmother Niú, the two-headed ox stumbled towards the crowd dancing by the river. Drunken laughter of different depths and tones echoed, fading as it reached the rippling waters of the river. The two-headed ox wanted to join but found her legs unfamiliar with the traditional dance steps.

"It will soon be our year," said Grandmother Niú in Mandarin. "But remember not to dip your head and body in the water when the sun rises."

The two-headed ox trotted towards the tree where Hǔ and their cubs lay alert, stacked: a large pile of orange fur with black stripes. Tù munched on rice cakes, their snow-white round tail shivering. Lóng and their descendants twirled around the tree with their red and gold scaled bodies wrapped around the branches, steamed fish held between their claws. Shé and their descendants slithered among the others.

The two-headed ox breathed in the familiar smell but found her appetite lacking. She realized there were no empty spaces for her to squeeze into, anyhow. She backed away from the crowd, heading for the field where Mǎ and Yáng grazed. Young foals and calves raced but paused to stare at the two-headed ox when she approached.

She tried to form words, but the sentences became muddled in her mind and the thought of speaking tied her tongue. *Perhaps another day.* She turned her back to the field.

In a plain clearing, Hóu, more human-like than the other animals, Jī, who clucked continuously, and their descendants traded red envelopes with barking Gǒu. The two-headed ox listened to the rowdy exchange. She did not have a red envelope to offer—only the one that her grandmother passed her, but that was for her to keep. She thought it would be intrusive to insert herself, especially empty-handed, and again turned from the gathering.

Zhū arrived last to the celebrations and fell asleep as soon as it finished its meal. The two-headed ox watched from a distance. Zhū's stocky body rumbled, and their large ears flew upwards, flopping with each breath they took. Zhū's silence was comforting, but still, the two-headed ox did not feel it was her place to join them.

"Why aren't you with the others?"

The two-headed ox turned and saw one of the Shu's descendants.

She shrugged.

"What's your name?"

The two-headed ox thought it was an unusual question to ask—most of the descendants carried the name of the original. But what was more unusual was when she realized that the Shǔ's descendant had spoken in English.

"Gemini," said the two-headed ox.

"Mouse," he offered in return. "I live on the other side of the river."

Gemini looked at the water, still rippling, occasionally splashed onto the grass of the two lands it divided.

"The West?" Gemini asked.

Mouse nodded.

"I return East during New Year."

It was the same for Gemini. New Year was the only time she saw her family. They had been adamant about not travelling West themselves though they pushed her to. A better future awaits you there, they had said.

"What about you?" Mouse asked.

"I was born here, but now I live in the river."

"The river!"

Gemini looked to the distance. Dawn was quickly approaching, and the New Year announced its silent arrival with a sliver of gold peaking over the horizons. The rest of the animals and their descendants were still asleep, but Grandmother Niú watched Gemini from afar, settled amongst the other animals.

"I must return home soon," said Gemini.

"You're not supposed to cleanse yourself today. It's bad luck."
Then after a pause, he added, "I'll come with you."

By the time they reached the river, the sun was directly above them. The other animals had awakened and gathered for their guests' departure.

Mouse hopped onto Gemini's back as her front foot dipped into the water, raising goosebumps on her pelt. It reminded her of her grandmother's words the night before. As Gemini's back foot left the land of the East, she felt the full weight of the river's current, one side rushing to the West and the other to the East, pushing against her body. Her legs trembled, but she withstood its force. Once she reached the middle, she paused and looked back. Grandmother Niú stood with a forlorn expression.

Most who chose to live in the river were washed away quickly. Sometimes, they stepped onto the land of the West without a second thought or stepped back onto the land of the East after further deliberation.

It was difficult to live in between.

Gemini looked around her. The water: a fragile balance of cultures pushed against each side of her body.

Mouse hopped off her back. His feet met the grass on the land of the West. As Gemini stood in the middle of the river with one head craned towards the East and the other towards the West, she began treading in place.

She was not yet ready to settle in the West, but she also knew she could no longer stay in the East. She had spent so many years in the West that the East was no longer familiar. But the East and its traditions were still rooted deeply within her, though buried and often difficult to reach until Grandmother Niú reminded her of who she was near the end of each year.

Although it was the Year of the Niú, she knew that this year would be as difficult as the others.

*Previously published in Flash Fiction Magazine.*

### *AUTHOR NOTE*

There are two things connected to human identity, for those who believe in their importance, that always fascinates me: horoscopes and the Chinese zodiac. I thought it would be interesting to explore both of these things in relation to my own identity in one story, and this flash piece was the result of that. I often feel like I'm two people in one—or sometimes even several to several hundred people in one—and it's both an interesting yet confusing and tiring experience. Maybe one day I'll feel like only one person, but then again, would I regret wishing for this merge?

# A Day of Mourning

Tea tasted sweet or bitter depending on Heyuan's mood, though she made it the same way every evening.

It was bitter on this day of mourning.

The teaspoon clicked against fine white china decorated in blue ink. The pattern looked different to Heyuan. Today, it looked like a dragon. The steam danced in a similar shape to the cup's design, dissipating under Heyuan's chin. It was usually comforting, but this evening, it made it harder for her to breathe.

Ancestors never showed when they were requested, but they understood when they were needed most. She thought of the tea dragon as her ancestor and released the breath she was holding.

Chinese opera floated in from the window, the high-pitched voice occasionally drowned out by... she wasn't quite sure what. It didn't matter anyhow. It was only background noise to Heyuan. She didn't bother trying to listen to the words. Lingering attachments would only make leaving more difficult.

Heyuan's tea sat untouched today.

There was a knock on her door. The tea was long since cold. The dragon flew elsewhere. Soon, she, too, would fly elsewhere.

Heyuan already withheld for as long as she could, but her home here would no longer exist the next week. She poured the tea down the sink and left the china. She would not bring it with her.

AI JIANG

*Previously published in Every Day Fiction.*

### *AUTHOR NOTE*

Leaving things behind is always difficult, and with this piece I wanted to capture the last moments before leaving happens—the quiet, the odd sense of peace, the melancholic atmosphere, the mind's unconscious desire to hold onto the past and never let it go, but eventually we do, and sometimes, we don't look back.

# Jinli Yu

Before they took you, we were watching the stream ripple as the gentle breeze caressed its surface. We tied our ox to a dove tree next to where we were sitting by the edge of the water. This was the time of day I loved most—when you and I stopped by the river on our way home from a long day in the maize field during harvest season.

Though we work the land, we do not own it. And though we have private thoughts, we do not own our bodies. Huangdi owns all.

It was the first time you told me about jinli magic and the first time you showed me your true form. At that moment, Father, you were more magnificent than Huangdì with your inked fins moving with the water, scales catching in the sun.

My feet dipped into the water, cool against sunburnt skin, and drifted to the left from the pressure of the current. My fingers fiddled with my straw-weaved sandals tossed beside me. The water looked deeper, darker today. Your face looked overcast, though the sun had not yet started setting, and there were only a few clouds, but they were barely there and sat almost translucent against the blue of the sky.

You took off your clothes and folded them neatly, placing them beside me before diving into the rippling currents of the stream. It was so sudden I could do nothing but stare, my hands cold like the water. Your body morphed into one much smaller, magnificent white with black ink: a jinli yu. The magic intrigued me, but only for a moment, because with a sudden change the currents became too strong, too violent for you to swim against. It carried you away as you thrashed, or was it only pretend? Your fins disappeared in a flurry of white.

My bare feet kicked grass and dirt behind me as I scrambled after you. I stumbled several times over the uneven ground below the mountains. You told me that magic could not be used unless you are calm. I wondered if you were calm while you were carried away. And if you were, why did you not come back?

When you disappeared too far for me to follow, I returned to where your clothes lay and hid them in the bushes near the stream. You would need them when you found your way back.

I whispered into the water: *I wish for your safe return.*


You never taught me the jinli magic. How could I follow you?

I now return to the place where you left me and whisper daily into the water. I know there is little chance you can hear me, but the water always has its way of carrying a message. Water travels far greater distances than our bodies.

The villagers murmur about how Huangdi is paying high prices for those who can bring him jinli yu because jinli symbolizes wealth, power, bravery, and such, based on its colour. I wonder, Father, are you brave? You never told me what each of the colours means.


If someone found you and took you to the palace, you were no doubt fluttering under the waterfall, as you often do when you needed to be alone. You never noticed, but I always knew where you were because that is where mother disappeared.

You told me that jinli yu could swim up waterfalls, but only those brave enough, strong enough, determined enough. You are convinced that mother is at the top. I know this was not true, but you would not believe me. She could not be on the top of the waterfall because I saw her red-scaled body drifting downstream, luring the collectors away from you while I hid in the forest until you found me. We don't blame one another; we only blame ourselves.

Father, you cannot find her over the waterfall. But perhaps you already know and that is why you jumped into the water that day even though the currents were unsafe. Did you want Huangdi's collectors to find you?

The villagers tell me that the jinli festival will be hosted at the palace soon, at the end of the year. Huangdi will release all the jinli yu he has collected in his pond. Jinli yu, the people like you and me. Will you return then?

I whisper to you again through the water, the trickle of the stream, the currents. My whispers are disruptions to the calm stillness in the middle of the night. I whisper my words to the currents in hopes they will carry my thoughts to you, but it is difficult when I am whispering upstream. The downward currents are unkind. But all the streams surrounding the villages lead to Huangdi's pond, though iron bars are blocking where the water flows outwards from the palace.

I return to our spot by the stream and place my clothes by yours in the bushes. My naked body cuts through the water, and I pray I am capable of magic before I hit the rocks at the bottom. I see the rocks and graze past them as the currents carry me downstream. Where others pray for opaque water to hide their colours, I hope, like Mother, I will be eye-catching enough to draw attention.

Wait for me, Father.


You told me that no one is born free. Freedom cannot be earned, but often bought instead. True freedom, you said, does not exist. Are you free in the calm waters of Huangdi's pond? When will you forgo the illusion of calm of the artificial pond and return to the irregular, rushing currents that carry you to the rest of us? The waters like the fields we tread against daily, feeling almost a sense of contentment in the struggle, rather than floating downstream with ease. For us, the struggle is normal.

When I think about your glassy eyes and inked scales when you disappeared, I understand why you never believed in true freedom. But unlike you, I believe it exists even if we must sacrifice our humanity for it, much like how Huangdi sacrifices his humanity for wealth and power.

You said what makes us different from the nobles and the royals is not our magic but our values: we value hard work; they value unearned wealth.

You told me we become spirits when we can no longer turn human again. But even spirits must battle against the winds that threaten to carry them away.

When they find me by the waterfall, whispering the names of both you and mother, I know I will meet you soon. But will you still be there, or will you have become a spirit?

As the festival continues and the nobles sway, drunk with wine, our tails cut through the pond's still water. We make it look so weak compared to the rushing streams in the mountains. But this freedom feels false, unnatural, constructed. Unsatisfactory. Unearned. There cannot be freedom without the struggle. But Father, you believe you have struggled enough.

I watch you swim, aimless, in the distance near a small waterfall. A waterfall that is hand-crafted rather than natural. It is smaller than the one you usually visit near the mountains. Your inked body thrashes against the current that is keeping you from climbing the fall while the rest of us dance in the calm water, not because that is what Huangdi wants to see, we dance because we can. It is only during this festival where we can believe that we are somewhere else, someone else, even if it is only for a moment. And only a moment is enough.

Father, why do you struggle to remain the same, but in a different place?

When the festival concludes, all the jinli yu, including myself, gather by the iron bars where the pond connects to the outer streams. With a booming laugh, Huangdi calls for the guards to open the pond gates. I now understand that he does this only so he can catch us again the following year when we most desire rest, when we no longer desire to swim against the current.

Without effort, the downward current pulls us along the stream once we are outside the palace walls. I turn back and catch sight of you, still trying to swim up the hand-crafted waterfall. Alongside the other villagers, I leave you behind. Once a safe distance away from the palace, each jinli transforms back into their human forms and climb out of the water one by one. They wave to the rest of us after fumbling to pull on the clothes they hid.

Father, you cannot stay at the palace forever.

I lean back on my hands at our usual spot by the stream with my feet cutting through the calm water. It has been almost a year since the festival, and I have been hard at work, harvesting the crops in the maize fields. Do not worry Father, the crops that you left behind are thriving.

The festival is approaching again. The palace men take my harvests to Huangdi, leaving me with only enough to survive. Sometimes, I think about the jinli magic, and you under the waterfall at the palace, but I know I will not hide my clothes by yours and enter the water again.

No matter what jinli yu I had become last year, our magic is only meant for a temporary rather than permanent solution to our daily, mundane battles. We cannot swim up waterfalls with magic alone.

Perhaps next year you will return. *And Father*, I whisper into the water, *I will wait at the top of the waterfall*. Turns out mother is already there like you said, but only you, Father, could never figure out how to get there. You were never brave enough to let go of the past. No matter how hard you swam against the rapids of the fall, you made no progress. To find Mother, we have to let her go.

When I raise my face from the water, I see a dragon jinli yu with swirling colours symbolizing bravery, strength, and deter-mination, dancing where my reflection should have been.

Soon, I will join Mother on top of the waterfall, while you, Father, continue to flutter at the bottom.

*Previously published in Luna Station Quarterly.*

## *AUTHOR NOTE*

I've always wanted to write a story about a shapeshifter, but the question was always, which one? I thought about the numerous shapeshifters that are commonly used, and none of them resonated with me and what I wanted to do with the piece. I seem to always come back to themes of water—flooding, drowning, waves, seas, lakes, oceans—so I knew it would have to be a creature of water. But I didn't want it to be a creature of vast water per-se, serpents, mermaids, and the like, but one of more contained, calm, yet rushing, waters. And so came ponds, and there followed jinli yu—or otherwise known as koi fish. They have such powerful colouring and symbolism, each different patterned fish symbolizing something completely different—wealth, bravery, reproduction. They're always caught and contained in ponds for these very reasons, to bring fortune to humans. But what if they were part human, what if they didn't want to be contained, and what if, they had a say?

# Questions
# From
# Between

# WRITING

**You write across a range of different styles and genres, is there a genre you're interested in that you have yet to tackle?**

Humour. Everything I write is more on the dark side of the spectrum, or more light-hearted, whimsical, and hopeful in nature, but I don't think anything I've written can be truly considered as humour. Growing up, I wanted to be a comedian at some point, and I love to make people smile and laugh, but to do it intentionally in the written form isn't something I'm great at. But like horror, humour is very subjective, though I'd love to try my hand at the genre at some point. I wrote a short "humorous" banter between two characters about virgin olive oil dressing, but we won't talk about that *shields face and runs away*.

**When do you write, and do you write every day?**

I write like chaos, like a wild mess—I think that's the best description. I don't always write every day because there are often other tasks I need to tend to, but I try to write in long marathons every other day when I can. Currently, I'm doing barely any writing I'd say after starting the Odyssey Workshop, which has taken up most of my time, and catching up on some planning stage things which there will be more news about soon! But when I'm more actively writing, sometimes it'll be from 10am to around 6-7pm, or it might be 12pm to 5pm, or sometimes it would be 9pm to 9am. I don't really have a set routine, I'd say. I usually end up writing until my brain tells me that my productivity for the day has come to an end.

**Do you prefer to plot out a story first, or just grab an idea and run with it?**

Until now, I've mostly been grabbing ideas and running with them, but with longer form, that's no longer possible for me. I'm trying my hand at plotting my stories out first so they're more coherent. I often have an issue with not introducing information at the right times, so plotting has been helping me with that—or at least I'd like to think that's the case.

**What is your favourite part of the writing process? What is your least favourite?**

The idea brewing process would be my favourite. The longer I brew on story and book ideas, the more the interesting tidbits appear and the more nuanced the story itself and the characters become. My least favourite would be revision, mostly because I often struggle with letting specific ideas go if I'm having trouble thinking up alternatives that will fit in with the rest of the narrative to replace what I had deleted or taken out already.

**You've also worked as an editor, do you think that has helped you as a writer at all?**

I definitely think it's helped me as a writer because it makes me more aware of the pitfalls that are common among short fiction but also because when you have to read a lot of submissions, you become more aware of what is commonly seen in each genre and how to explore common concepts and ideas differently.

**Do you have a piece of your own work that you're particularly proud or satisfied with? Why?**

I think *Linghun*, my debut novella, is something I'm proud of most. It brings together everything I've commonly explored in my writing and aspects of my own personal experience, but also what I have learned as a writer so far in my career in a coherent (at least I hope) whole.

**Where does a story usually start for you? Is it a concept, a character, a feel, or something else??**

I'm a big fan of concepts and coming up with new and lesser seen concepts. It's the passion to bring these ideas to life that drives me.

**Do you let anyone read your stories before you submit?**

When I first began writing, I'd pass my work along to maybe 3-7 beta readers before I sent it out, but as time went it, it became unsustainable to do so because I'd also spend more of my time offering to beta read for two or three times the number of people who had read my work. Now, I'm been trying to learn methods of self-revision to save time, though I might send my long form out to beta readers still as it's a new beast for me to try to wrangle.

**Which part of your writing do you believe has strengthened the most as you've progressed over the last two years?**

I would like to say the emotionality and emotional resonance of my stories and the execution of the concepts I'm trying to explore, but I find that I often still lean towards the side of vague, and I'm trying to find a way to retain my voice and style but make my writing more accessible at the same time.

**What has been the key thing for you to be able to be so prolific over the past two years?**

There was a saying, though I can't remember who it was from now, that what you need most to help you achieve goals are passion, determination, and discipline. I suppose it is my passion for writing and storytelling that drives my desire to bring to life my story ideas as quickly as I can, but also to forward my career so that it becomes one that is sustainable.

**Do you have any advice for writers just starting out on their journey?**

Be kind, be flexible, be open to feedback, and stay passionate, determined, and disciplined.

# Baobei

Yijing's mother never woke before the sunset—mellow orange rays bled from the open terrace.

"Yijing, baobei," his mother drawled.

Her voice slithered across his skin, raising goosebumps as he approached his parents' bedroom, devoid of his father's presence for several months now. Yijing peered through the half-concealed entrance, door swaying, hinges creaking. His mother lounged on one side of the bed as though someone still occupied the space beside her. She raised a fresh cigarette to her lips, her eyes wide, unblinking. On the bedside table, smoke drifted from the ashtray where a recently tossed stub sat atop grey dust like a grave.

"That's her second pack today." Yijing's grandmother shook her head as she walked past, pausing only briefly to say these words to Yijing while obscuring the room's opening from sight.

At this moment, Yijing hated his father even more for leaving, though it was no fault of his own. Illness is always such an unpredictable thing.

Yijing's brows drew together at the sight of the wallpaper inside the room—flakes of yellow snow peeling from frayed paper edges, fluttering to the ground.

"Mother." His voice wavered. His left foot rose towards his mother's room, but he never placed it down. Instead, he skittered several paces back.

"Your father played the most beautiful songs on his guitar... Do you remember?"

How could Yijing forget? Between his parents' fights, his father's music was the only thing keeping peace. It was the only happy memory that lingered. Other recollections were all tainted by his father's pale face and blue lips.

"Could you play something?"

Yijing froze. His guitar had been collecting dust in the corner of his bedroom. He would cast it fleeting glances each day, but since his father's passing, the strings no longer sang.

"Baobei?"

Yijing left the front of his mother's room and entered his own, staring at the guitar from the entrance, feeling as though to approach would be to disrupt some kind of invisible peace.

He settled down in the living room after dusting off the lacquered wood of his acoustic Fender, remembering that the last time he touched the strings was next to his father at the hospital as his heartbeat slowed. As he turned each peg, every tested note sounded like a desperate cry, a scream of frustration, the unwavering note of the monitor when it realized the heartbeat was missing.

"Baobei?"

The Fender's cries drew his mother out of her room for the first time in a week.

Yijing no longer felt like a "baobei" even though his mother still called him such. And as his mother leaned against him, Yijing felt himself stepping into the shadow of his father as he ran his hand across the faded wood before the echoes of his father's favourite song beckoned his fingers to curl over the strings in rhythmic strumming.

Though Yijing's mother still held a cigarette between her fingers, the open window carried the thin trail of smoke outside. Stale air replaced with the fresh, breathing a tendril of life back into the pair. As Yijing continued the song, the strings sliced through his softened calluses, but he felt no pain.

"Sounds just like Laijing."

*Previously published in TL;DR Press.*

### *AUTHOR NOTE*

One death that has impacted my life immensely is my Uncle's death back when I was in the fourth grade. I was never close enough to make the judgement, but my family had always warned my uncle against marrying his wife. But to lose a husband, and to having a child who is stuck with you through the grief and mourning, could not have been easy. So this story is for my cousin, who has become such a strong man, albeit still chaotic and overly aggressive at times, and his mother, who I haven't heard from or much about in years.

# Missing Dolls Around The World

CW: Abuse, graphic imagery

They found the first coffin in North America, in Vancouver, BC, at a graveyard. The slender mahogany box was no larger than the forearm of a child of ten. The workers were digging a slot for the upcoming burial of an important political figure I was hired to cover. This was meant to be an historical moment, among the others I documented, but this one didn't seem as significant in comparison, and only perceived as such because of the politician's wealth and power, making his voice louder, more heard than others who lay voiceless in their graves around us. I wasn't there for the voiceless, but I should have been. Both the diggers and I were surprised when they unearthed the miniature coffin instead.

Within the coffin lay a molding doll with one eye missing dressed in plain black cotton smeared with specks of dirt. Where there should have been a black, plastic, void, there was instead a deep speckled green that spread across the rubber face like disease. Her raven hair, much like my own, was tangled, lank, clumped, and greasy—singed and split at the ends. Her toes were blackened, charred with darkness crawling up her legs like a living, growing shadow, though the doll herself was dead, as was the owner she resembled.

A cruel joke was what I hoped this was, as heavy droplets of sweat rolled down my back, catching at the waistband of my high waist jeans. The handle of a thin blade—sheathed—tucked at my side, tremored against my skin as I shook. It was probably unnecessary, but I could never be too safe. It was a risk being unarmed ever since the first time my ex breached the restraining order against him. It was lucky I only came away with a minor concussion. Staying in the dark for a week wasn't too bad, but missing the jobs I could've taken on, like this one, made a dent in my savings—a dent I couldn't afford.

I stood next to the workers as they continued to dust off the small coffin. My face scrunched up in a confusion that matched theirs.

"What is that?" I asked.

A young boy ran forth and snatched the coffin from the digger's hand—one of their sons perhaps; maybe it was take-your-kids-to-work day; what a great place for the boy to frolic—and clutched it with a grip so tight his bones showed through stretched translucent skin. If the doll were alive, it wouldn't be able to breathe between his fingers.

"Broken," the boy whispered with bulging eyes and a smile so wide it looked as though his face would rip apart.

I wondered where else might similar dolls be unearthed.


The second coffin was found in the basement of a condo set for demolition in Manhattan. Its waterlogged wood was consumed by murky mold from prolonged exposure to moisture and a lack of sun. The second doll was missing her legs. Her ginger hair sat in a messy topknot with her yellow cotton dress, embroidered with sunflowers, soiled beneath the hips. The doll's eyes were intact, but they looked tired, weary, defeated, with oval indents of purple weighing down the lower lids.

Second Doll's husband was a joy, on the outside, with a cigarette in one hand and the palm of his other digging into the small of her back at his annual company party. Her bright gold dress cost more than half her salary working parttime at the grocers as a cashier, but her husband forced her to buy it anyhow—a new one each year. The husband didn't want Second Doll to work full time and certainly didn't allow her to wear the makeup she had on now to work.

"There's no need... especially for a job like *that*," he had said.

Second Doll stayed. And she smiled. And she blinked back liquid pain that burnt the lower lids of her eyes, lining them red.

What else could she have done?

Her parents loved him, her friends loved him, she... loved him? Didn't she?

Yes, of course she did—does. There would be no one else more suitable, her parents had said, and she was running out of time. No one wanted a withered flower whose petals had begun falling. She was already twenty-five—the same age her mother had given birth to her. Yes. Second Doll *needed* him.

Second Doll didn't attend the next annual company party. Her husband didn't want her wearing a maternity dress; he wanted her to stay home: "It's better this way. You need rest, don't you?"

She caressed her growing belly and leaned back against the headboard of the bed, her legs elevated on pillows. Second Doll watched *The Great Gatsby* for the eighth time that month, knowing but denying that under similar dazzling lights of Gatsby's ball, her husband would be drinking wine with a woman not named Myrtle—but might as well have been.

"My love," Second Doll said in the French words her husband loved to hear from her lips before they married. He hung up after quickly telling her he was busy.

Did she want her baby to live with such violence?

I ripped the Second Doll's MISSING poster down from where it was posted on the chaotic announcement bulletin in the abandoned condo's lobby, the paper curling at the edges with a few phone number tabs pulled off. 212-XXX-XXXX. With the poster folded in halves, I put it inside my pocket. Was the phone number that of a family member, a relative, her husband, or maybe a casual lover who found themselves far too deep to leave, a Gatsby, or maybe someone like me?

The third coffin was found in a large sports field in Mexico City. Within the wooden walls slept the third doll with his eyes closed. Where his arms should have lain were limp bits of deflated grey fabric—grey because his mother wouldn't allow anything more vibrant, eye-catching, the neon that Third Doll loved.

"Why can't you be more like your father?" Third Doll's mother asked in English, slamming her kitchen knife down on the chicken, flesh splattering across the cutting board.

Third Doll bowed his head, hands tightened into fists at the sides of his body. He was fourteen, had only begun high school this year. Why must he carry the weight of his family, his mother's pain, the responsibility for his sister's future, in his barely calloused hands?

"You can be better," his mother muttered.

Indeed, he could. He knew he could. But with his mother reminding him daily that he could never be as great as his father, would he continue believing that better was possible? That to be *a man* was possible? What did it even mean?

As Third Doll's mother continued to grumble in Spanish, words they both knew he couldn't understand having been sent abroad for school until now, he couldn't help but imagine Lady Macbeth in the place of his mother. She was never satisfied. Even before his father had passed, she never did stop comparing him to more capable men, more traditional men, men who were *more Mexican*, and perhaps that was why he disappeared into the storm three years ago. Third Doll's grandparents sent his father to the States, and Third Doll's parents sent him to Canada. Why, if his mother would only complain about his whiteness when he returned?

And perhaps that was why Third Doll, too, would disappear three years later.

Though his mother had blubbered on the news article I read from the comfort of my home in Ontario, I felt the raging storm and the bone-chilling dampness that seeped through clothes and skin. And I imagined Third Doll trudging through heavy winds into a world of madness that might not be quite as mad as the one he'd left, even though it was dry and warm—though only physically.

Third Doll's mother was not unlike the relatives and strangers I've encountered, who always asked, "How can you not know Chinese if you're Chinese?" And all I could answer with was "I'm sorry," in English, before leaving them standing, open-mouthed, speechless. What else could I have said?

They didn't find coffins in Saskatchewan, but they found hundreds of dolls: each had a missing mouth—not so much missing as sealed with tight black stitches sewn across the lips. Each had on white cotton dressing, their original colour almost unrecognizable for the dirt stains ingrained into the fibres of the material. Hair, long and short, trussed or missing, hung down the faces of each doll, hiding their chips and scars.

The dolls watched from a distance the same way their parents watched them, their figures seemed more like shadows that could be mistaken as a brief wavering of the trunk of trees, a mirage, rather than a real presence. There was an unseen bridge the dolls could not cross—what their teachers and employers bestowed upon them were not enlightening teachings but vicious borders, chain-like boundaries.

They tried to whisper the words their teachers could not understand under their breaths. But the sound, so different from the dominant tongue, rang loud across the unspeakable school grounds.

"English, only," the teachers shouted.

The dolls slept amongst those like themselves yet learned from others who held completely different values, beliefs, traditions, and spoke a different language.

Unlike Coyote, the Trickster, the teachers had tamed the dolls, forced assimilation, created a neat uniform line of "model citizens" churned out like clone figures from a factory conveyor belt.

And the traditional songs, the culture, the words, the stories, stuttered, then stopped at the tip of the doll's tongues as foreign tones strangled and forced the muscle behind teeth, behind lips, to form words that caused their spirits to weep—for the mind knew what the body didn't: words could be as poisonous as hemlock.

But still, I stood at grounds where they unearthed the dolls, the horrors, the unburied, and lowered the camera in my hands, wondering how could they ignore, suppress, the truth of the unspeakable schools because they tarnished a history that was already tainted?

But there are also missing dolls elsewhere, not only in North America. In Edinburgh, near the towering, ancient volcano called Arthur's Seat, were seventeen murder dolls found by three boys in 1836.

The echoes of those dolls will remain as ghostly whispers, repeating the same question, "What will happen to me when I die?", and receiving the same answer: "You'll be sold for 7 pounds. For science."

In a particular museum, I found these dolls. The knife still tucked in my waistband warmed with my skin. I ran my fingers over the leather sheath, and beneath, the plastic body of the handle.

Who knew where other missing dolls might be, and what parts they might be missing, or whose hands they may still be in. Sometimes not knowing was better, or so I told myself, but I needed to know—I had to know.

And where these dolls, the missing humans, were buried, well, their lives may have been far more gruesome than their graves—though those were often equally frightening.

If I hadn't left the house and my rather handsy family when I had, would there have been a doll of my own? These missing dolls, perhaps, I could help them with my words.

I unsheathed my knife, a different one, a fountain pen, and buried the tip into my notepad, my eyes never leaving the coffins in the museum display cases. Each one was different yet the same, but each held my gaze captive, begging me to hear their silent plea and warnings for the other living dolls in North America and across the world. Though it was not my story to tell, I wanted to listen to their words with my own. We were all connected, both the living and the dead—dolls with our tongues missing.

*Previously published in The Dark.*

### *AUTHOR NOTE*

This story was originally written in second person, at least the parts of the narrator were. But many asked why it had to be in second, and it was something I too readily changed when challenged about the choice. Thinking back, I think my intention had been to have the narrator feel like they are not themselves when they're on the job, having to report on various deaths without being too emotionally connected to them, even if the struggle is futile in the end.

This story was also inspired by the discovery of the famous murder dolls in Edinburgh. Though not specifically about the dolls, when I wrote this piece, it was during a time of death and turmoil when there were news circulating concerning the unmarked graves found in residential schools across Canada.

# Hunting Season

CW: Brief graphic imagery and violence

National Park 3065's law enforcement team imprisoned Likenst regularly, but only for a night. The laws on hunting aren't too strict.

I spent nights sneaking him pieces of imitation jerky, tossing them through the bar openings. Sometimes it wouldn't reach Likenst's hands, toasted by electric currents rippling from the metal instead. My eyes followed the meat. It hissed before landing on the ground.

"It's better burnt," he said. "Tastes more like real meat." The last time he tasted anything close to real meat was a few years back when he was still employed at the conservatory.

Likenst and I headed to what was previously a national park, now recreational hunting grounds for leisure. We used to have set hunting seasons each year, now every day was "hunting season"—a joy when work became stressful but hunting with Likenst was stressful by itself. Regardless, I had to deal with him since he was my uncle.

"Please, keep an eye on him," said Likenst's wife, Margery, while balancing their child on her shoulders. A pained smile on her face. I felt the guilt of responsibility. Though I had turned eighteen only a few months previously, I often felt much older than Likenst, who was twice my age.

"I'll try." My tone was far from confident, and for good reason.

Likenst was already in their family's hovercraft. His head plunged into the backseats as he tossed his daughter's toys into the storage area.

"You can tell what he puts first." Margery continued muttering to herself as she pressed the button to close the door.

I noticed her "what" instead of "who".

I offered a small wave and encouraging smile as the steel door slid shut.

"I think Margery wants you to stay home more often."

Likenst chuckled. "Trust me, my presence at home doesn't make much of a difference."

Before I climbed into the passenger seat, Likenst closed the many notifications that popped up on the large screen beside the wheel, obscuring the navigation system. I caught a glance before he wiped the screen clean. Unpaid bills.

My great grandfather left us a message complaining about meat. We didn't have that anymore—only man-made imitations were available now. It didn't taste too different. Likenst had a taste of fresh meat, oven cooked, once.

Animals still existed, but not where they were easily accessible like before. We had a conservatory for them.

When we arrived at the National Park 3065, named after the year of its construction, Likenst rubbed the back of his neck as we pulled up to the front gate. Tall trees peeked from the top of the walls lined with barbed wire. I wasn't sure whether it was meant to keep the animals in or the humans out. The animals were unlikely to escape; they're programmed to remain within the walls. A swallow blinked at me from a tree. A flash of red from its eyes glinted in the sun.

I passed Likenst my work ID, knowing that his ID had long since expired. He waved it across the verification scanner.

"Welcome back, Lynn Zhao." The words appeared with a picture of my face, unsmiling.

"Thanks." Likenst didn't meet my eyes.

"Don't mention it."

Likenst floated the hovercraft above two others when we pulled into the parking area. Our feet met landing platforms as soon as we stepped out. Likenst pulled our equipment from the back of the craft. We didn't need it, but it never hurt to take precautions.

"You should get a craft too."

I pulled on the rebound suit. If anything—beast or human—were to charge at me with less than friendly intent, the suit's force field would propel them backward. I'd never had the chance to experience it.

"Maybe when they're fully reliant on solar fuel."

Likenst shook his head.

Likenst loved going for the quick herbivores. I usually stuck to the carnivores.

When the small pellet of my shooter—similar to the laser pointer at my workplace—met its first target, I jogged over and stroked the mane of the lion that lay motionless on the ground. On the side of my shooter, a small "4" flashed. I removed the pellet and popped it back into the shooter. As soon as the pellet left the lion's body, its circuits rebooted, propelling its mechanical body off the ground. Its muscular form rippled as it plunged back into the bushes.

"Lynn."

I watched the lion disappear before heading towards Likenst's voice. My body froze when I entered the clearing. Likenst stood over a brown and beige body with his shooter's pellet, bloodied, pinched between two fingers.

"It's a deer."

I recognized it from the records my great grandfather left behind. "What is it doing here?"

"Isn't it gorgeous?"

Gorgeous wasn't the right word for it. I looked away from the deer. Blood trailed from the right eye socket where Likenst had shot it. When we shot the robots in the eye, they'd only short circuit or malfunction. Shooting the eye was a habit of Likenst's that always placed him in the park's prison. Sorry, Margery, I failed again.

I frowned. "How did it get here?"

"I guess this one must've missed the transportation craft."

The expression on Likenst's face suggested he was lying. His lips twitched upwards, though his brows furrowed.

"What are the chances we can sneak it out?" he said. His eyes were hungry, and his lips were parted slightly.

Likenst raised the pellet to his nose. The deer's only eye met mine. Its body trembled with laboured breaths.

Margery appeared in my mind. Her eyes rimmed red like the deer as the doors closed, similar to the closing door of the oven that cooked the deer Likenst snuck home from the conservatory.

"Likenst."

When he turned, my shooter's pellet found its way to his eye.

"I much prefer the hyenas over deer."

National Park 3065 security imprisoned Likenst, again. This time, he would remain.

In the back of a hovercraft, I stroked the deer head resting on my lap as we headed towards the conservatory. I munched on dried vegetables and offered a piece to the creature beside me.

*Previously published in TL;DR Press.*

## *AUTHOR NOTE*

Concerns regarding the environment and endangered species, whether animals or plants, have always been on my mind. And in this story, I wanted to explore what it would be like if all species on earth were endangered and placed in conservatories, but sports such as hunting still persisted.

# Questions
# From
# Between

# READING

**What are your fall time favourite books/authors?**

I don't find my reading particularly influenced by the season I think, but some newer works that I've enjoyed recently include Clay Chapman McLeod's *Ghosteaters*, Naben Ruthnum's *Helpmeet*, Cassandra Khaw's new collection *Breakable Things*, and Kelsea Yu's *Bound Feet*.

**Who do you think are the most interesting recent authors working in genre fiction?**

Oh there are far too many to name so I'll only drop a few: Somto Ihezue, Hannah Yang, Elaine Boey, Isabel J. Kim, Marisca Pichette, Venezia Castro, Steven Gonzalez, among others!

**Do you typically read in particular genres, or do you hop around all sorts of books?**

I'm a big fan of reading as broadly as possible, but I have to say my first love is very historical tinged literary fiction, memoir, with horror, fantasy, and sci-fi mixed in between!

**What inspires your work, beyond the work of other authors?**

Life, news articles, random historical or futuristic research I do, movies, shows, artworks, or even single words.

**If you had to choose just three stories of your own, long or short, that you think would best encapsulate you as a writer, which would they be? (And where can they be read!)**

Oh, that's tricky... I'd probably say "Give Me English" in the May/June 2022 issue of The Magazine of Fantasy and Science Fiction, "Where the Grass is Always Whiter" forthcoming in Interzone Magazine, and "Tooth, Teeth, Tongue" in the February 2022 issue of The Dark Magazine.

**Tell us a handful of the current must-read short story mags/journals in your opinion?**

Outside of the well-known few that have been around for quite some time, I'd say Hexagon, Solarpunk Magazine, Tales From Between, The Deadlands, Tree and Stone, The Dread Machine, khoreo, Dark Matter, Haven Spec, Apparition Lit, If There's Anyone Left, Radon Journal, Orion's Belt—I'm sure I'm missing many other great magazines!

**Is there a story you've read that you wish you had written?**

When I first began writing, there were a lot of things I wished I had written, but now, there isn't, because those aren't my stories. All the ones I've read are stories that only those writers can write, and I have stories that only I can write.

# Waves and Seesaws

I t was Xiu's first time going to No Frills alone.

Xiu picked up her red wallet with intricate, traditional Chinese designs sewn onto its surface, closed shut by two small, golden metal balls that snapped together. She clasped her weathered hands together and held them up to her forehead. There were lines etched into her leathery skin. She stood and prayed in front of her closet. Then, she grabbed her thin, royal blue fall vest, and pulled on old woolen gloves just in case the wind was chillier than expected.

Xiu's son would not be home until well past ten, maybe eleven, and his wife would be back around nine, but that was highly dependent on the train she had to take from downtown back up to Scarborough. Luckily, or perhaps unluckily, she only had to cook for herself and her two granddaughters, who she would have to pick up from school in two hours. That meant she had an hour and a half to go to No Frills and head back.

The old woman pocketed her old watch—the strap of one side had broken off, but she refused to replace it—before she made her way to the front door. Right when she opened the door, the phone rang, but she decided to leave it; usually, the children answered the calls before their parents returned. Xiu slipped on the worn cloth shoes she'd brought with her from her home in China before she locked the front door behind her.

Once Xiu cleared the pathway in front of her son's house, and reached the end of the driveway, she took an immediate right.

Rather than focusing on the scenery around her, she counted her steps with care until she reached the first street opening that led her out of the neighbourhood. As she neared the main road, she saw the cars rush by; occasionally, the cars slowed and turned into the neighbourhood. Xiu stared straight ahead even as the cars holding neighbours who might know her drove past in the opposite direction.

Xiu took a look at the neighbourhood street sign: A tall letter topped with a flat hat, two short ones that followed after, a letter that resembled a backwards music note that her granddaughter's piano score was littered with, two short ones again, the backwards music note once more, two more short ones, and it ended off with a sideways scissor. She shook her head and decided to call it 'waves' because that was how it would look if she drew a continuous outline over each letter.

Xiu took a right after she passed the sign. The last time the whole family went to No Frills on the weekend, her son turned left on a street that started with a snake shape and ended with a music note with two dips in between. Xiu concluded that 'seesaw' would be a fitting name for this street. When she saw the sign for seesaw, she turned left.

When Xiu finally arrived at No Frills, the back of her sweater stuck to her skin, and her sweat had soaked through its holey fabric and drenched her vest. She was worried that others would be able to see the colour difference.

With her head ducked low, she walked as quickly as her feet would carry her into the grocery store. Xiu contemplated grabbing a shopping cart but quickly decided against it as it would slow her down and potentially draw more attention to her. After all, she only needed an item or two to make dinner. The rest she had at home.

Xiu headed for the produce section of the store and searched for the cabbage because that was the closest thing it had to the choi found in Chinese supermarkets. Then, she made haste towards the meats section, careful to avoid the shopping carts that disrupted her path and the eyes of other shoppers who may have been criticizing her for blocking their way.

Once she picked up what appeared to be chicken breasts, Xiu marched towards the cashier with her two items in hand. After observing each of the checkout lines, Xiu took her spot behind an elderly man with a cane; the location of the checkout lane was conveniently next to the exit.

"That will be $10.50," the cashier—a young woman perhaps twenty-five in age—said in English.

Xiu's throat suddenly tightened and dried. She tried to keep a confident smile while she reached inside her vest pocket for her wallet, but her hands shook as she unclasped the twin metal balls that revealed the coins and paper money that sat within. Xiu stared hard at the folded bills and circular pieces of metal.

"Mam—" the cashier began, but Xiu, with a sudden panic, raised her head and freehand, waved both frantically and shut her wallet before running out of the store. Sweat broke on her forehead, and her cheeks felt inflamed. Xiu did not stop walking until No Frills was well out of sight, leaving 'seesaw,' the chicken breasts, and cabbage behind on the metal packing surface beside the cashier.

After she picked her grandchildren up from school, which was only one street away from the house, Xiu set out to cook dinner while the children watched T.V. There were only eggs and steamed fish from the night before left in the fridge. Xiu sighed but resigned to work with what she had on hand.

When both granddaughters settled themselves down at the dinner table, the eldest said, "Fish, again? Why can't we have something else?"

"Don't waste food. Just eat it," Xiu reprimanded the young girl in Chinese but felt a sense of guilt stirring within her empty stomach.

The younger of the two siblings paid little attention to the exchange between her older sister and grandmother, humming the new words she had learned in English in kindergarten that day in a made-up song. The younger granddaughter's song was interrupted by a shrill ring, which immediately caused her to drop her chopsticks and scramble towards the phone. The eldest rolled her eyes and continued to eat with a scowl.

"Sorry! My parents aren't home right now," said the younger sister before she placed the phone back in the receiver and bounded back into the kitchen.

Xiu stared at the little girl in awe and even chuckled to herself as she continued eating.

The next day, Xiu decided that she would try going to No Frills once more.

The elderly woman prayed in front of her closet, grabbed her small wallet and watch, but abandoned her vest and gloves this time. She brushed her hair back from her face and secured it in place with crisscrossed bobby pins on each side before heading for the door.

The phone rang right after Xiu had locked the front door, but in manic haste, Xiu unlocked the door and ripped it open, flying through the entrance towards the phone before the caller on the other end exhausted their patience.

"Sorry!" Xiu shouted quickly before ending the call.

The single word filled her with a newfound sense of confidence and determination. For some reason, she knew that she would return home with the cabbage and chicken breasts this time as she closed the door behind her once again, passing waves and towards seesaw.

*Previously published in HAD.*

### ***AUTHOR NOTE***

My grandmother is an immensely headstrong woman who survived a plague when she was a child—one that took away her entire family and most of her village. Since arriving in Canada, she hasn't taken to the language or the landscape. She doesn't often leave the house, but when she does, she never strays far, and usually only to places where she knows there are people who speak her mother tongue—Fuzhounese—or at least Mandarin. But on rare occasions, she experiences a moment of bravery and she might endeavour English-speaking stores, though in real life, she'd usually only go when someone else in the family is present. As children, me and my sister loved my grandmother very much, but we were far too ungrateful and far too unsympathetic. Thinking back, and even now, she is the strongest women I've ever met.

# That Is Earth

The Mountains look shorter today. Perhaps this means hope, but maybe not.

"Grass."

I look back to see my friend tumbling down a Hill nearby.

"Grass," he calls again as he climbs the small Hill atop which I sit.

"What's the matter, Tree?" I ask the tall figure looming over me.

"Look what I found," Tree says and holds up a circular object covered in vibrant greens and blues and flecks of white.

"What is that?" I take the object from his hand and hold it up to take a better look.

"I asked Owl and she said that it's Earth. It's the place we live on," Tree says in an excited tone.

"Earth," I whisper and lower the sphere.

I look at the Mountains in the distance with their blurred texture. The sharp and round edges of electronic boxes both small and large create a jagged ascent to the top of the Mountain, which no one has yet attempted to reach. At least, not to my knowledge.

"Isn't it neat?" Tree says in awe as he takes Earth back into his own hands and cups it between two palms.

"Neat?" I test the word in my mouth. "Maybe not."

Tree looks up from Earth and meets my eyes with confusion but remains silent, then, he abandons his new discovery on the ground between our feet.

"Where is Flower?"

Tree and I turn to see Owl scaling up the Hill. As she nears us, she leaves a trail of dirt and shoes tumbling with every step she uses to propel herself upwards.

"Eating, I suppose," I say after a moment.

Owl frowns. "At this rate, she will finish the Fill by herself."

Tree snorts and laughs. "Are you sure she hasn't already?"

I stifle my laughter.

"Crow should be with her," I answer the silent question that Tree does not ask.

"Great, they won't leave us anything good," Tree says and suddenly jumps up.

He blocks what little sun threatens to scorch my jaded skin.

"Stay there," I say.

"I'm not going to shade you all day." Tree rolls his eyes.

I shrug. "Couldn't hurt to try."

"Come on," Owl hoots. She is already descending the Hill; this time she is following the trail of tumbling worn heels, sneakers, and broken sandals.

Tree and I follow, careful not to entangle ourselves in the loose laces and straps, and the occasional string of connected Velcro footwear that has lost their other half. I look back to see the abandoned sphere of green and blue on top of the shoe Hill before catching up with Tree who is now carrying Owl upon his shoulders. Owl turns her head to make sure I am still there.

Upon arriving at the Fill, we hear the tinkling of high-pitched giggles. I stop in my tracks to duck as something whizzes over my head. A rotten apple rolls to a stop a few paces away. Tree and Owl laugh, but I shake my head in dismay. Flower can be such a child, and though Crow is supposed to be a good influence, this is not the case.

"Hey!" Tree calls to the two that are hidden from sight on the other side of the Fill.

The top of a head appears, and Crow's sleek black hair follows as the rest of the head and the body emerges. Two slender arms appear immediately after, stretching and revealing the rest of Flower's flexible limbs as she jumps up from her spot.

"Save us anything good?" Owl asks as she takes large strides up the Fill towards Flower and Crow, ruffling Crow's hair once she reaches him.

Crow frowns at his sister while he straightens his hair that now sits askew. Flower pulls a dusty, half-eaten cob of corn from her pocket and hands it to Owl and then tosses two bottles of dirt speckled water to Tree and I. This water is cleaner than the bucketful that Flower found last week. I take a swig and marvel at the clumps of damp mud that run down my throat.

"Cheers," Tree says as he extends his crumpled, plastic bottle towards mine.

I smile. "Cheers."

I watch as Crow skitters around the Fill, snatching up bits and pieces of food scraps between his slender, claw-like fingers and then tossing them into the air before catching the pieces in between sharp teeth, dry lips. I begin to walk over to him to offer my water, but Owl stops me.

"Don't bother," she says.

I shrug and sit where I was standing. The sky is darkening as we finish our meal. Though we cannot see the sun, we know that it is setting behind the grey smog that covers the sky.

As the first drop of rain reaches the uneven ground, the five of us scramble for cover. Under a canopy patched together by Tree using pieces of tarp and duct tape, we sit huddled against one another in a line, watching as the rain drenches the Fill, the Hill, and the Mountains in the distance.

Crow is the last to make it under the canopy, and before he sits, he tries to shake the water out of his hair. Owl glares at him as he splatters water on her skin but remains silent rather than lecture him the way she usually does. Lightning flashes beneath the thickness of the grey sky above us.

I retrieve the buckets from the back of our canopy and place them in front where the tarps end. When I sit back down, I notice the small ball of green and blue in the distance on top of the Hill. I try to focus on its colours, but when the rain starts to fall quicker and heavier, the Earth tips over the edge of the Hill and tumbles down, rolling out of sight as the rainfall draws a curtain over the landscape in front of us.

*Previously published in Haunted Waters Press.*

***AUTHOR NOTE***

With growing landfills and issues of trash and litter, this story imagines a world where landfills have become uncontrollable, covering all of the lands on earth. Through the eyes of the surviving life on earth, but humanized with the readers' ability to hear their thoughts, I wanted to show the detriments and consequences of the path we could very well be heading straight for, and the homes we would be robbing, not just from other humans, but from everything still living.

# In The Eye of the Observer

There was only thirty minutes before Una's reallocation appointment, but it was just enough time to talk to the Babbler—the elderly woman had a real name but never stopped talking long enough to say it, or maybe she didn't want to. It was a dream to become an Allocation Artist like her mother, who played a large part in the creation of the Allocation System.

Though her mother's physical presence no longer roamed in the home Una used to share with her, her ink blot paintings covered the walls of every room. Still, she wondered where her mother had been transferred to, having had no contact with her over the past three years. Perhaps as an Allocation Artist, she could speak with her mother again.

"Una! Lovely as always to see you. You look more like your mother every day," the Babbler said. She wrung her hands in front of her, the wrinkle lined fingers mixing with the swirling black and white patterns on her shirt—the same patterns that hung on Una's walls at home, and the same patterns as the graphic art displays at the Allocation Center.

"Yes, yes, lovely," Una said in a rush.

Though the Allocation Center was only a five-minute walk from Una's house, being tardy for a reallocation appointment would mean waiting another three years and an increased likelihood of ending up with an undesirable allocation. It was strange how the Babbler never booked a reallocation appointment when her three years were up but renewed her contract instead. How enjoyable could work as an Allocation Quota

Tracker possibly be? It seemed the position was driving the woman mad, though the elder's presence in Una's neighbourhood was quite useful.

"Anything new with you lately?" Una asked. Her eyes darted to the cameras nestled at the top of each streetlight, the lenses no doubt focusing on their encounter—Neo Kertian eyes, watching, listening.

"Nothing new, as usual, but you know how it can be. The bugs are always annoying—never seem to be rid of them completely." Openings for Exterminators. "I'm always burning my hands when I'm cooking. Sometimes I wish they'd create automated cooking machines!" There seemed to be an increased demand for techies. "And there isn't enough space in the backyard for my dogs." Land Laborer shortage. That was no news. There was always a shortage of Land Laborers. When these allocations required such a high level of physicality, workers were sure to burn out quickly.

"You know what I need more in my life, though? Artwork. My walls are so barren. I wish I was an artist. Don't you?" The question caught Una off guard. The Babbler had never asked questions during their previous interactions. An opening for an Allocation Artist?

Before she had the chance to reply, a Supervisor staggered down the street towards them, clearly unworried about being caught wandering from his station. It was ironic for him to suddenly take an interest in his job when he called to Una and the Babbler. "Hey! Why—Why are you young ladies standing around?" His red, swollen eyes made the sunken, purple grooves on the Babbler's face more pronounced.

The Babbler shrinks into her hollowed shirt, flimsy in the breeze.

"We never have enough of those Supervisors." The Babbler's sarcastic tone brought a smile to Una's face.

"Never enough." Una nodded in agreement.

"The things I'd do to become a supervisor," the old woman mused, then her face sobered and she shook her head. "Perhaps not." Her eyelids folded together, leaving only a sliver as she trained her irises on the middle-aged man before eyeing the cameras. "You know, back thirty years ago in 2105, before the Allocation System. Accountants and Job Recruiters like my parents were—" She held her hand up, a high bar.

Una did know. The Babbler never failed to mention her background each time they met. Everyone understood how important family trees were—yet, for Una's previous two allocations, she was never allotted the role of Allocation Artist—and they all understood how chaotic Neo Kertian was when the labour market collapsed in 2105 until the creation of the Allocation system. Now, there was a dual celebration of Neo Kertian Day and Allocation Day—a day Una's mother was never home for.

"Anyhow, my... grocery list beckons me. I have... deadlines to meet and many things I need to pick up... for others." The Babbler winked before strolling back to her house.

"Allottee number fifty-six, Una Yin," a disembodied voice called. The words bounced off the walls of the waiting room. There was an eerie calmness to the low-pitched tone that never failed to unsettle Una.

A previously unseen door slid open, revealing a similar white box with seemingly endless walls. Soon, at eye-level, an illusionary graphic ring appeared around her, a few steps away in each direction, like old film strips. Connecting slides appeared. Unique ink blot images hovered side by side.

The voice followed Una into the room. "You may begin."

Though the images already brought to her mind thoughts related to art and design, Una worried it might wander elsewhere—to insects or cooking utensils or worse, dirt and land. Some tried voicing their desired allocations during the appointments, musing about their dreams of becoming Actors, CEOs, or for some, Exterminators, but the Allocation Artists and Observers never paid mind to those. Only what the eyes and mind revealed was taken into consideration. Of course, that was only Una's guess. No one was allowed to reveal the details of their allocations—not even to family.

When Una returned to the waiting room it only took a minute before the voice returned.

"Allottee number fifty-six, Una Yin." A pause. "New allocation: Allocation Artist."

Hope welled up within Una. Perhaps this would bring her closer to her mother.

Una never realized that being allotted certain allocations meant you were no longer able to reallocate again. Was that why the Babbler remained an Allocation Quota Tracker? Would she herself remain an Allocation Artist? Would it give her enough time to find her mother?

After arriving at the Allocation Center, Una entered from a hidden entrance on the opposite side of the main doors. In the Allocation Artist's control room, two figures—one hunched, one upright—sat in front of eight screens stacked in two rows. Una was told to stand in the back and observe for the first day.

"Allottee number sixty-eight, Konite Lunet."

Una's fingers twitched as she attempted to resist the urge to run them over the control board lit up with multiple-coloured squares. It was not the art that Una was used to seeing her mother do at home—the canvases and buckets of ink that disappeared slowly over the years—but it was fascinating none the less.

Screens in front of the current Allocation Artist pulsed with shifting graphics, morphing inkblots. The Observer next to the Artist watched the allottee wandering the allocation room, making note of where they paused and the specifics of the images they took an interest in. The Artist pushed specific buttons, morphing the images as the allocation continued. Thoughts of the allottee flashed across the Observer's screen: images, words, phrases—most interconnected. Una's heart thrummed faster every time the allottee paused at an image, remembering her previous two allocations.

When the allottee left the room, the Observer submitted the data into the system.

"Pay close attention," said the Allocation Artist. A hacking cough escaped her lips.

Una watched as the results popped up on the screen, lighting up the Observer's face. *Techie.* Una smiled. A wonderful job.

The Observer pulled up on a different screen. With fingers moving quickly across the keyboard, the Observer wiped *Techie* off the results bar and inserted *Land Laborer*.

Una's tongue dried. She turned to the Allocation Artist.

"Why did they change it?" Her voice quivered.

"There's a shortage of Laborers." The Artist shrugged.

"But there are also open spaces for techies," Una said, recalling the Babbler's words. She watched as the allottee's expression fall when his allocation was announced.

"Perhaps, but some are favoured over others for the role... Even if they are not the most qualified." Una's mind could not help but flit back to the Supervisor.

When the Allocation Artist left holding a handkerchief to her jaded face, Una turned to the Observer, who looked far less affected by her work.

"Does that happen often?" Una asked.

"Yes and no," said the Observer.

"Yes, and no?"

"We get a list of the upcoming allocation or reallocation appointments for the day. Some are marked red—the ones I must change—while the others remain as the results appear. Sometimes, no one is marked on the list."

Una remembered the Babbler's *grocery* list, and she thought of her mother and how she had worked in this field for as long as Una could remember.

"Who decides the list?" Una asked. She had a feeling what the answer was, but she wanted to make sure.

"I... I'm not sure. We're not told. The list is already here before I arrive each morning," the Observer said.

"Can we change the marked results back to their original?"

"That... has never been attempted, but I am sure it would be illegal."

But to Una, the list itself seemed far more illegal—or at least unjust.


A month into her new allocation, Una was slouching her way to the Allocation Center when the Babbler appeared in front of her, forcing her to a halt.

"Something... wrong?" the Babbler asked.

"I need to get to work," Una muttered. When she stepped to the side, the Babbler mimicked her movement.

"How about some... tea at my house after work?" The Babbler's eyes flitted towards the cameras and back to Una, holding her gaze.

Una paused, then nodded.

"Tonight then."


When Una arrived at the Babbler's house, she wiped her hands on her black slacks. Not only were there cameras around the streets but also inside buildings—commercial, government, *and* residential.

"Come in, Una," said the Babbler when she opened the door. A man was in view behind her on a leather couch, scrutinizing Una from a distance.

"Don't mind my husband. He is always a little... grouchy, you could say."

Una offered a small smile. The Babbler's eyes flew past Una before she beckoned her inside. Once the door closed, both the Babbler and her husband released a visible breath. The elder woman pulled a small remote from behind her back.

"I'm Maryum, in case you were curious." There was no longer a cautious tension around the Babbler when she said this. "Don't worry. The house is soundproof."

"Maryum," Una said repeated, still unsure what to make of the situation.

"Yes, Maryum."

Maryum's husband Josiah led Una and his wife to a small room hidden behind the kitchen cabinets. "Bedrooms and basements are too obvious a hiding place, don't you think?" Maryum said.

"How?" Una asked. Her hands trembled, and she dove her hands into her pockets.

"Old tech," Josiah said.

Una nodded in realization. Her mother hoarded old tech in their basement until they took both her and the tech away. The government couldn't bug the old tech, so it became illegal, *dangerous.*

"His allocation...?" Una asked when she saw the display of screens in the small room, cameras of their own. Her eyes widened when she noticed one screen on the bottom. In the living room sat Maryum, Josiah, and Una, having tea.

"Techie. I'm not sure how long it will be before they find us out, but for now, we're safe." Maryum placed a hand on her husband's shoulder. "Show her."

Josiah switched three of the screens at the top. The Land Laborer Fields. Una leaned closer, rising on the tips of her toes. The man Konite stood with a shovel in his hands. Maryum passed Una a headset.

Konite slammed his shovel into the unrelenting soil. "Does this ever get easier?" he asked.

Ruben mimicked Konite's action, but with less brute strength, more precision. "Yeah. Just strike at the right angle," he answered.

"The right angle? And what would that be?" Konite watched in amazement as the hard dirt ground crumbled beneath the dulled end of Ruben's shovel. "Surely it would be easier for them to hire someone who already has the know-how. I don't feel like I'm of use here."

Ruben wiped the sweat from his upper lip, then flicked the perspiration to the side, shrugging. "By feeling."

Konite sucked his lips inwards, grumbling. "They should just get machines."

Ruben offered a cheeky smile, a muddy dimple indenting his lower cheek and another on the side of his chin. "But then there wouldn't be jobs for people like us."

"Which allocation is this for you?" Ruben asked.

"My first." Konite took the chance to catch his breath, leaning against his shovel, watching Ruben work effortlessly. It was a wonder that Ruben survived fifteen years of this. The air clawed at Konite's throat. If his father were here, there wouldn't be a need for such heavy physical labour.

"Bummer. This is my fifth allocation. They never give me a different one. I come from a family of Land Laborers, so it isn't so bad. What allocation were you hoping to get?"

"Techie," Konite said. He tried to concentrate his thoughts on images of innovation and advancements and the technical skills his father passed onto him in secret before the Neo Kertian government took him.

"Just a secret between you and me... no one here seems to get anything different when they reallocate. Some disappear from the field... I don't think it was from the reallocation though."

Konite scrambled off his shovel when a Supervisor stumbled by before realizing the woman couldn't see straight anyhow. He flicked his eyes toward the woman. Ruben shook his head and mouthed, *the job isn't all dazzles*. Then, Ruben cleared his throat, speaking as though he never stopped. "Bummer. You get to know a person and then poof! I'm surprised I'm still here."

Konite wondered what secrets Ruben were hiding, pretending to be unaware even though he could see it was only an act. But the more persistent issue at hand was how long would Konite last as a Laborer.

"What did your father do?" Ruben asked when the workday ended.

"He went to prison after they found him with old tech."

"... Bummer."

"Old tech?" asked an unfamiliar voice.

Konite and Ruben turned. A woman approached, a labourer like the two, with an aged smile. Both men snuck a glance at the Supervisor. The woman waved a hand.

"Don't bother with her. We all know she won't notice. They don't place cameras here, anyway. They're not too worried about us."

How could this woman know so much? Konite narrowed his eyes. "Who are you?"

"The Founder of the Allocation System," she said, handing him a small device.

When Una headed to work the month, the discovery that her mother was still alive instilled only one thought within her: today was the day she would rebel against the system, even after Maryum had cautioned her. She had waited long enough, even if she were to be caught, Maryum would not be associated with her action—at least that was what she had hoped.

Una arrived half an hour early, just so she could stare at the control panel in disgust. There had been a handful of allottees with business and government official parents destined for the life of a Land Laborer but allocated office allocations instead.

There was only one allottee left for the day. Una prepared herself mentally to prevent the Observer from changing their allocation.

"Allottee eighty-five..."

Rather than watching her own screen, Una tracked the allottee's thoughts on the Observer's screen from the corner of her eye. Swirling within her mind was anger and hatred for the Allocation system and her desire for its destruction.

Before the Observer could change the allottee's result from *Techie* to *Land Laborer* like they had done to Konite, Una threw herself over the Observer and pressed "announce results".

Maryum stood outside the Allocation Center when they came to take Una to the Land Laborer Site. In her hands sat a stack of clothing, grey like ashes. Maryum passed it to Una, slow and careful.

While Ruben hacked away at the land they needed to clear for the new neighbourhood, Una drew shapes in the dirt that resembled the ink blots she constructed as an Allocation Artist, watching it swirl under her feet as she destroyed the images with her shovel when a Supervisor neared.

"Don't bother. They never notice," Konite said, his tone absentminded.

Hidden within the folds of the clothing Maryum passed Una was a small chip and a piece of paper with Konite's name scribbled on top. Konite seemed completely consumed by what he held in his hand after inserting the chip inside.

To Una, it seemed like a camera or communication device of some sort. It reminded her of the screens in the control room and the cameras that lined her neighbourhood. Though the device in Konite's hand eventually turned on with the screen illuminating his face, the Supervisors paid no attention as they staggered with no specific purpose or direction in mind.

Finally, Una abandoned her shovel and approached Konite's crouching figure.

"What is that?" Una asked.

Konite, eyes still glued to the illuminated screen, opened his mouth. "Hope." But it was not his voice that left his lips but that of Una's mother's.

### *AUTHOR NOTE*

This is one of the stories I struggled to place, written in early 2021. It never felt complete, but I never ended up expanding it. I wanted to include it to remind myself of how far I've come as a writer, but also how far I still have to go. And if anyone is interested, they can peek at the struggles of early writer Ai. The intention of this story was to explore what a dystopian society would look like if our careers were chosen through Rorschach inkblot art. I must say, my earlier sci-fi is a mess that focuses solely on the concept rather than the characters. I'd like to say I've improved, but I'm still trying to figure out the balance between effective worldbuilding and the development of interesting and emotional character arcs.

# Linghun
# (Excerpt)

*Linghun is the first long piece of fiction by Jiang to be published (April 4, 2023 by Dark Matter INK).*

*What follows is a tantalising taste of her debut novella.*

## WENQI

I stumble dizzy and carsick into the kitchen to find Mother unpacking. Her eyes dart everywhere rather than focused on the task at hand. Bowls and plates litter the island, the dining table, and the edges of the sink. Cupboards sit open, empty. Father stands next to her, rubbing a hand across his stubbled chin, running a finger along a growing shadow of a mustache. His other hands rests against the sink, twitching, not knowing where else to place it or what he should be doing with it.

"The agent said it might take a while before he appears," Mother says in a feverish whisper, fixing her hair the way she used to right before leaving for a job interview.

Before we got the house, she worked in a travel agency down-town. But that didn't last long. Mother said there was a new co-worker who too closely resembled what my brother would have looked like as an adult. Their names were also similar.

"In the pamphlet she gave us, it says placing their items or photos around the house might help," Father says.

Mother flings herself over to a box by the fridge and rips it open. She takes out several framed family photos—none are recent. All the pictures, like my brother, are frozen in time. Mother hurries around the house while Father and I stare. She places one frame on the dining table and one on the coffee table in the living room. Her footsteps thunder up the stairs. Doors open, close, open, close. Footsteps pitter, patter, pitter, patter. She returns, and I imagine she has placed a similar family portrait on the desk in my room: Mother, with her hand on my shoulder, the other hand on my brother's, Father behind her with a hand at her waist and the other on my brother's head.

When Mother returns, she grabs a stack of unframed photos, this time of *only* my brother: ultrasounds, preschool and kindergarten pictures, him in a graduation cap, holding a certificate of excellence at the end of first grade. His photos end there. A younger me, half my brother's age, stands in the picture, clutching his arm with a wobbly smile and missing teeth.

My brother was always the golden child, the one who carried the family's honor, the one who would carry the family name as per tradition—unlike me, who will only carry the name of my husband *if* I were to marry. Mother and Father often try to convince me that they are not as traditional as their parents, yet they doted on my brother, the first-born son, and often forgot about me. They still do, even though he's gone. I'm convinced that, had they been offered the choice, my parents would have traded my life for my brother's, with little hesita- tion. At least, Mother would have, and probably still would, if given the chance. I grew up hearing her complain often how Father's Mother was always insisting that my parents try for another son, but Mother was—and still is—too heartbroken to think about children.

Mother disappears again. Father and I wait, listening to the ticking of a small clock—the same one Mother would use for my brother's reading hours, back when we still lived in Fuzhou. I still remember the way my brother drew me closer while he read so that I could see the words, but they were always too advanced for my age. I can recall the images, but I don't recog- nize the Chinese characters in my memories.

After Mother sets everything up, the three of us sit in the living room waiting for something to happen—for my broth-er's promised appearance—but nothing does.

## MRS.

The new arrivals to the neighborhood moved into the house across the street.

There is only one reason anyone would trek through the guarding trees to get to HOME: not to seek new life, but to satisfy a longing for the dead.

Houses in HOME sate the unending hunger of those most vulnerable, unsuspecting. They feed on our desires, our pain. So much pain. And to wallow in such pain...It is a hideous thing.

Isn't it strange? How everyone here desires their homes to be haunted?

You wonder if the newcomers will be the same as the others. You wonder if they, too, will be unrelenting, or perhaps they will be like you... unhaunted.

## WENQI

After we eat dinner in silence, I move to the living room window and look out upon our new street. Our lawn is overgrown and full of weeds, but it is also full of

people. I had been too sick on the drive in to care much about these odd vagabonds, but curiosity gnawed at my mind.

"Why are there people on the lawns?" I ask.

"Don't worry about them," says Mother, sounding more than a bit absentminded. "The agent assured us that these people are a normal occurrence here, since everyone wants to move into this neighborhood and is more than willing to wait. What did she call them again? Oh yes, *lingerers*—that's the word. But it matters not. We're just grateful we got a house here. Aren't we?"

I look out again at the trees that have grown too tall, too unruly for the narrow street. Their overgrown branches cast ominous shadows over our house and the rest, preventing any sunlight from reaching the roofs or shining through our windows. This house resembles little of our home in Scarborough, and it's nothing like our home back in Fuzhou.

Father looks to Mother. His grip tightens against his chopsticks, and his knuckles turn white. "Yes, yes, yes," he agrees.

Most of the neighborhood is unkempt, but directly across the street, a plain little home rests upon a neatly trimmed plot of grass. Cared-for flower beds line the house's front facade. Above the tangles of rose and lavender, I see an old woman sitting by her own front window, clutching an urn upon her lap. Instead of drawing the curtains closed like I expect her to, she continues to stare at me and my family.

I turn back to my parents, speaking again of the people on our lawn. "Can we ask them to leave?"

"No," Father says, eying Mother through a mask of worry.

Back outside, a man leans against the large SOLD sign stuck into the grass. Below it is the neighborhood's name in a smaller bold font: HOME—Homecoming Of Missing Entities. It sounds like a joke, but nothing about this place feels worthy of laughter. Mother has a smile on her face, but Father seems more wary about this endeavor.

The lingerers continue to stare at the house, *into* the house, with their bodies almost leaning towards the front door, as if being manipulated by an unseen pupeteer and their invisible strings. The lingerers on the other lawns hold the same position. My parents pretend to not be bothered by it, but I can see the sweat glisten on Father's forehead, and I can see Mother discreetly wringing her hands, playing with her wedding ban. A boy sitting on the lawn two houses down, across the street, has his back turned to the brown and yellow house he sits in front of. His eyes catch mine, and I can see a spark of curiosity.

I wonder how long the boy has been here. And I wonder when I will be able to leave.

***End of Sample***

### *AUTHOR NOTE*

I'll leave everything to be said about *Linghun* to the novella itself. I've included a personal essay with the book, and I hope that everyone will put their trust in me as a storyteller and grab a copy if it piques their interest.

Order your copy directly from Dark Matter here: darkmatt ermagazine.shop/products/linghun

# Questions From Between

# MOVING FORWARD

**How ambitious are you in your career as a writer?**

I try to be as ambitious as I can, so at least if I fail, I can say I've tried. With that said, I'd love to have my work be made into movies or TV shows, or perhaps even comics. I want to have written either fifty books in my lifetime, or perhaps half that number—but to be truly and utterly passionate about each of those works.

**If a film/TV show were to be made from any of your works, do you think you'd want to be involved as the screenwriter, or would you be happy for others to take over?**

Honestly, I think screenwriting is a whole different beast from short stories and novels. I'd like to try it someday, but until I can deep dive into the craft of it, I don't think I'd want to take on the screenplay conversion myself. I'd love to have a say and play an active role in production processes (or even a very minor role). To have a hand in some part of the process, I think, for now, would be enough for me!

**You're transitioning into longer pieces, novellas and novels, do you think short form writing will still have a place in your future?**

100%! Short stories are the first loves I can never let go of, and hopefully, editors will continue to think of me for anthology invitations, so I have an excuse to run to the short story world to procrastinate on my novellas and novels...

**What are you working on right now?**

Too many things, yet nothing at all. That's to say I'm not actively writing everyday but doing a lot of things that are writing related—solicited shorts, blurbs, reviews, research, and lots of future project planning. But in terms of works in progress, I'm trying to put together two novels, one of which may or may not end up becoming a series, a different tetralogy, and a novella—maybe a second novella for a duology if the one I have going on submission with my agent soon gets picked up!

**You can get anyone alive to blurb your next book, who is it and what do they say?**

Neil Gaiman, and I'd imagine he'd say something along the lines of "I can't tell what's stranger: the world of the novel or the writer".

**You turn seventy and look back on your writing career, what would you like to have achieved?**

There are too many things I'd like to achieve, but to mention some of my previous goals, it'd be 25+ books, the Hugo/Nebula/Aurora/Stoker/World Fantasy/etc award or nomination, movies/TV shows of my works, and the big whale dream of a seven-figure deal. But most of all, I suppose one thing that all writers would love to have achieved is the victory over imposter syndrome. Though I have to say, having it has been more of a virtue than a vice for me, I think, as it pushes me to continue honing my skills as a writer and never settle when there is always room for improvement.

# Thanks

"To everyone who has read and supported my words, always encouraged and believed in me, thank you, thank you, and thank you again! "

*Ai Jiang*

# More To Read

**FURTHER EDITIONS OF TFBPRESENTS:**

Elin Olausson's Shadow Paths

Samantha Kolesnik's Lonesome Haunts


**OTHER RELEASES:**

Tales From Between: A Strange Literary Journal

Tales From Between: Words & Pictures


**SUPPORT TFB:**

Join our Patreon and never miss a thing we publish: patreon.c
om/TalesFromBetween

Our Patreon also acts as an eBook subscription
to our publications.

www.ingramcontent.com/pod-product-compliance
Lightning Source LLC
Chambersburg PA
CBHW020931160726

47993CB00005B/2230